MY FIRST
NURSERY
COLLECTION

to Zoë, Kate, Alex, Pip, and Saff

This hardback collection first published in 2013 by Andersen Press Ltd.,
20 Vauxhall Bridge Road, London SW1V 2SA.
Published in Australia by Random House Australia Pty.,
Level 3, 100 Pacific Highway, North Sydney, NSW 2060.

My Favourite Nursery Rhymes first published in 2007 by Andersen Press Ltd.
Copyright © Tony Ross, 2007.

My First Nursery Stories first published in 2008 by Andersen Press Ltd.
Copyright © Tony Ross, 2008.

10 9 8 7 6 5 4 3 2 1
British Library Cataloguing in Publication Data available.

ISBN 978 1 84939 500 7

MY FIRST NURSERY COLLECTION

Retold and illustrated by

TONY ROSS

ANDERSEN PRESS

CONTENTS

THREE BLIND MICE

Three blind mice, three blind mice,
See how they run, see how they run.
They all ran after the farmer's wife,
Who cut off their tails with a carving knife.
Did you ever see such a thing in your life,
As three blind mice.

PUSSY CAT, PUSSY CAT

Pussy cat, pussy cat, where have you been?
I've been up to London to look at the Queen.

Pussy cat, pussy cat, what did you there?
I frightened a little mouse under her chair.

"MIAOW!"

SING A SONG
OF SIXPENCE

Sing a song of sixpence,
a pocket full of rye,
Four and twenty blackbirds,
baked in a pie.

When the pie was opened,
the birds began to sing,
Oh wasn't that a dainty dish
to set before the King?

The King was in his counting house,
counting out his money,
The Queen was in the parlour,
eating bread and honey.

The Maid was in the garden,
hanging out the clothes,
When down came a blackbird,
and pecked off her nose.

RING-A-RING O' ROSES

Ring-a-ring o' roses,
A pocket full of posies.
Atishoo, atishoo!
We all fall down.

THE THREE BILLY GOATS GRUFF

ONCE upon a time there were three Billy Goats, who lived in a peaceful valley far away.

They were called Big Billy Goat Gruff,

Little Billy Goat Gruff

and Baby Billy Goat Gruff.

One bright spring day, Big Billy Goat Gruff said, "I think we should move to the other side of the valley. The grass looks much greener over there."

His two brothers thought this was a good plan, but to get there, they had to cross a rickety old bridge, under which lived a great big, mean Troll, who loved nothing better than a tasty little Billy Goat for his supper.

Baby Billy Goat Gruff was the first to bravely set off across the bridge.

"Trip, trot; trip, trot!" went the rickety old bridge.

"WHO'S THAT trip-trotting over my bridge?" roared the fearsome Troll.

"Oh! It is only me, Baby Billy Goat Gruff."

"Well, I'm going to gobble you up!" roared the greedy Troll.

"Oh, no! Don't eat me! I'm much too little," said Baby Billy Goat Gruff. "Wait for my brother, Little Billy Goat Gruff. He'll be along in a moment. He's much bigger!"

"Well, be off with you then!" roared the Troll crossly, and Baby Billy Goat Gruff scuttled across the bridge to safety just as fast as his little baby hooves could carry him.

Then, his slightly bigger brother, Little Billy Goat Gruff, started across the bridge.

"Trip, trot; trip, trot!"
went the rickety old bridge.

"WHO'S THAT trip-trotting over my bridge?" roared the fearsome Troll.

"Oh! It's only me, Little Billy Goat Gruff."

"Well, I'm going to gobble you up!" roared the greedy Troll.

"Oh, no! Don't eat me!" said Little Billy Goat Gruff. "Wait for my brother, Big Billy Goat Gruff. He'll be along in a moment. He's much bigger!"

"Well, be off with you then!" roared the Troll furiously, and Little Billy Goat Gruff scampered across the bridge to safety just as fast as his little hooves could carry him.

Finally Big Billy Goat Gruff started across the bridge.

"Trip, trot; trip, trot! Trip, trot; trip, trot!"

went the rickety old bridge.

"WHO'S THAT trip-trotting over my bridge?" roared the angry and by now very hungry Troll.

"It's me! BIG BILLY GOAT GRUFF!"

"Well, I'm going to gobble you up!" roared the greedy Troll, and with that he lumbered up on to the bridge to do just that. He was so heavy that the bridge creaked and groaned under him. But Big Billy Goat Gruff was a match for any Troll. He butted him hard in the bottom and tossed him high up into the air.

The startled Troll spun round and round and round, and then fell –

do_w_n

do_w_n

do_w_n

with a great

BIG

SPLASH!

– into the river below, and was never heard of again.

And as for the three Billy Goats, they lived contentedly to a ripe old age, munching the green grass on the other side of their peaceful valley.

TWO LITTLE DICKY BIRDS

Two little dicky birds sitting on a wall,
One named Peter, one named Paul.
Fly away Peter, fly away Paul,
Come back Peter, come back Paul.

THREE LITTLE KITTENS

Three little kittens they lost their mittens,
And they began to cry.
"Oh mother dear, we sadly fear,
That we have lost our mittens."
"What! Lost your mittens, you naughty kittens!
Then you shall have no pie."
"Miaow, miaow, miaow, now we shall have no pie."

28

The three little kittens, they found their mittens,
And they began to cry.
"Oh mother dear, see here, see here,
For we have found our mittens."
"Put on your mittens, you silly kittens,
And you shall have some pie."
"*Miaow, miaow, miaow,* now let us have some pie."

The three little kittens put on their mittens,
And soon ate up the pie.
"Oh mother dear, we greatly fear,
That we have soiled our mittens."
"What! Soiled your mittens, you naughty kittens!"
Then they began to cry.
"*Miaow, miaow, miaow.*" Then they began to sigh.

The three little kittens, they washed their mittens,
And hung them out to dry.
"Oh mother dear, do you not hear,
That we have washed our mittens."
"What! Washed your mittens, you are good kittens,
But I smell a rat close by."
"Miaow, miaow, miaow, we smell a rat nearby."

WHAT ARE LITTLE BOYS MADE OF?

What are little boys made of?
Snips and snails and puppy dogs' tails.
That's what little boys are made of!

WHAT ARE LITTLE GIRLS MADE OF?

What are little girls made of?
Sugar and spice and all things nice.
That's what little girls are made of!

SEE-SAW MARJORY DAW

See-saw Marjory Daw,
Johnny shall have a new master.
He shall earn but a penny a day,
Because he can't work any faster.

THE ENORMOUS TURNIP

ONCE upon a time an old man planted a turnip. He carefully tended over it, watering it regularly and shading it from the hot sun. As the months passed, the turnip grew . . .

and grew ... and grew until ...

... it was enormous!

"It's time we pulled that turnip up!" said the old man's wife.
"I'll make a delicious turnip soup for our dinner."
So the old man went to pull the turnip out of the ground.
He pulled . . .

and he pulled . . .

and he pulled . . .

but no matter how hard he pulled, he could not pull the turnip up.

"Come and help me, wife!" he called. "I can't pull the turnip out of the ground!"
So the old woman pulled the old man and the old man pulled the turnip.

They pulled... and they pulled...

and they pulled...

but no matter how hard they pulled, they could not pull the turnip up.

"Come and help us!" they called to their neighbour. "We can't pull the turnip out of the ground!"
So the neighbour pulled the old woman, the old woman pulled the old man and the old man pulled the turnip.

They pulled... and they pulled...

and they pulled...

but no matter how hard they pulled, they could not pull the turnip up.

"Come and help us!" the neighbour called to his son. "We can't pull the turnip out of the ground!"

So the son pulled the neighbour, the neighbour pulled the old woman, the old woman pulled the old man and the old man pulled the turnip.

They pulled... and they pulled... and they pulled...

but no matter how hard they pulled, they could not pull that turnip up.

"Come and help us!" the son called to his dog. "We can't pull the turnip out of the ground!"

So the dog pulled the son, the son pulled the neighbour, the neighbour pulled the old woman, the old woman pulled the old man and the old man pulled the turnip. But no matter how hard they pulled, they could not pull that turnip up!

"Come and help us!" the dog barked to the cat, who was sitting watching them. "We can't pull the turnip out of the ground!"

So the cat pulled the dog, the dog pulled the son, the son pulled the neighbour, the neighbour pulled the old woman, the old woman pulled the old man and the old man pulled the turnip.

They pulled...

and they pulled... and they pulled...and–

– out of the ground came the turnip and they all tumbled backwards in a great big heap!

All that pulling had made them very hungry, so they pushed
and they heaved and, at last, they managed to shove
the enormous turnip into the house.

The old man's wife cooked up a delicious pot of turnip soup,
and they all sat down together to enjoy the feast!

JACK SPRAT

Jack Sprat could eat no fat,
His wife could eat no lean.
And so betwixt the two of them
They licked the platter clean.

THERE WAS A CROOKED MAN

There was a crooked man,
Who walked a crooked mile.
He found a crooked sixpence,
Upon a crooked stile.
He bought a crooked cat,
Which caught a crooked mouse,
And they all lived together
In a little crooked house.

THIS LITTLE PIGGY

This little piggy
went to market,

This little piggy
stayed at home.

This little piggy
had roast beef,

This little piggy
had none.

And this little piggy went,

"WEE wee wee,"
all the way home.

I HAD A
LITTLE HEN

I had a little hen, the prettiest ever seen,
She washed up the dishes and kept the house clean.
She went to the mill to fetch us some flour,
And always got home in less than an hour.

She baked my bread, she brewed my ale,
She sat by the fire and told a fine tale.

PETER PETER PUMPKIN EATER

Peter Peter pumpkin eater,
Had a wife and couldn't keep her.
He put her in a pumpkin shell,
And there he kept her very well.

HENNY-PENNY

ONE day Henny-Penny was pecking up corn in the farmyard
when a small conker fell from a nearby tree and –

WALLOP! – hit her on the head.

"Goodness gracious me!" exclaimed Henny-Penny.

"The sky's going to fall down!

I must go and

tell the king!"

So off she set,
and soon she met
Cocky-Locky.

"Where are you going, Henny-Penny?"
asked Cocky-Locky.

"I am going to tell the king the sky's falling down,"
said Henny-Penny.

"May I come with you?" asked Cocky-Locky.
"Certainly, Cocky-Locky," said Henny-Penny.
So Henny-Penny and Cocky-Locky set off to tell the king the sky
was falling down.

Soon they met Ducky-Daddles.

"Where are you going, Henny-Penny and Cocky-Locky?" asked Ducky-Daddles.

"We're going to tell the king the sky's falling down," said Henny-Penny and Cocky-Locky.

"May I come with you?" asked Ducky-Daddles.
"Certainly, Ducky-Daddles," said Henny-Penny and Cocky-Locky.

So off set Henny-Penny, Cocky-Locky and Ducky-Daddles to tell the king the sky was falling down. Soon they met Goosey-Poosey.

"Where are you going?" asked Goosey-Poosey.

"We're going to tell the king the sky's falling down," said Henny-Penny, Cocky-Locky and Ducky-Daddles.

"May I come with you?" asked Goosey-Poosey.
"Certainly, Goosey-Poosey," they said.

So off they all set to tell the king the sky was falling down, and soon they met Turkey-Lurkey.

"Where are you going?" asked Turkey-Lurkey.

56

"We're going to tell the king the sky's falling down," said Henny-Penny, Cocky-Locky, Ducky-Daddles and Goosey-Poosey.

"May I come with you?" asked Turkey-Lurkey.
"Certainly, Turkey-Lurkey," they said.

So off they all set to tell the king the sky was falling down, and soon they met Foxy-Woxy.

"Where are you going?" asked Foxy-Woxy.

"We're going to tell the king the sky's falling down," said Henny-Penny, Cocky-Locky, Ducky-Daddles, Goosey-Poosey and Turkey-Lurkey.

"Oh, but this isn't the right way to the king's palace," said Foxy-Woxy. "I know the quickest way. Shall I show it to you?"

"Yes please, Foxy-Woxy!" said Henny-Penny, Cocky-Locky, Ducky-Daddles, Goosey-Poosey and Turkey-Lurkey.

So off they all set to tell the king the sky was falling down, and soon they came to a small, dark hole. This was really the door to Foxy-Woxy's cave, but Foxy-Woxy said to Henny-Penny, Cocky-Locky, Ducky-Daddles, Goosey-Poosey and Turkey-Lurkey,

"This is the short cut to the king's palace. Follow me and you'll soon be there."

"Thank you, Foxy-Woxy," said Henny-Penny, Cocky-Locky, Ducky-Daddles, Goosey-Poosey and Turkey-Lurkey.

Foxy-Woxy went into his cave, and turned round to wait for the others to come in. Turkey-Lurkey went through the dark hole into the cave first. He hadn't got far when –

SNAP! – Foxy-Woxy snapped off Turkey-Lurkey's head.

Then Goosey-Poosey went in, and – SNAP! – off went her head.

Then Ducky-Daddles waddled down, and – SNAP! – off went her head too.

Then Cocky-Locky strutted down into the cave, and hadn't gone far when – SNAP! SNAP! – went Foxy-Woxy.

The first snap missed Cocky-Locky, so he had time to call out to Henny-Penny, "Go back! Go back!"

Henny-Penny turned tail and she ran off home just as fast as she could, and so that was why she never did tell the king that the sky was falling down.

LITTLE JACK HORNER

Little Jack Horner sat in the corner,
Eating his Christmas pie.
He put in his thumb and pulled out a plum,
And said, "What a good boy am I!"

ONE, TWO, THREE, FOUR, FIVE

One, two, three, four, five,
Once I caught a fish alive.

Six, seven, eight, nine, ten,
Then I let it go again.
Why did you let it go?
Because it bit my finger so.
Which finger did it bite?
This little finger on the right.

LADYBIRD, LADYBIRD!

Ladybird, Ladybird!
Fly away home.
Your house is on fire,
And your children are gone.
All except one,
And that's little Ann,
For she crept under
The frying pan.

POLLY
PUT THE
KETTLE ON

Polly put the kettle on,
Polly put the kettle on,
Polly put the kettle on,
We'll all have tea.

Sukey take it off again,
Sukey take it off again,
Sukey take it off again,
They've all gone away.

OLD
MOTHER
HUBBARD

Old Mother Hubbard,
Went to the cupboard,
To get her poor doggie a bone.
When she got there,
The Cupboard was bare,
So the poor doggie had none.

MARY, MARY

Mary, Mary, quite contrary,
How does your garden grow?
With silver bells and cockle shells,
And pretty maids all in a row.

THE
GINGERBREAD MAN

ONCE upon a time there was a man, and his wife, and their young
son, who all lived together in a cosy little house. One sunny
morning the woman made the young boy a Gingerbread Man.
She put it in the oven to bake, and said to the young boy, "You
watch the Gingerbread Man while your father and I pick some
apples in the garden."

So the man and his wife went out to pick the apples, and left the little boy to watch the oven. But the little boy didn't watch it all the time, and all of a sudden he heard a noise. He looked up and –

POP!

– the oven door popped open, and out of the oven jumped the Gingerbread Man.

"You can't catch me!"

laughed the Gingerbread Man, and he ran out of the open door, down the steps and into the garden.

The little boy ran after him just as fast as he could, but he couldn't catch up with him. He called out to his parents, and they gave chase too.

But they couldn't catch the Gingerbread Man either, and he soon disappeared out of sight down the road.

The Gingerbread Man ran until he came across two men digging the road. They looked up from their work and called out,
"Where are you going, Gingerbread Man?"
And the Gingerbread Man laughed as he raced past and said,

"I've outrun a man and his wife, and a little boy and I'll outrun you too-o-o!"

"Oh, you will, will you? We'll see about that!" said the men, as they threw down their spades and ran after him too.

The Gingerbread Man ran on until he met a big, grizzly bear, who was looking for honey.

"Where are you going, Gingerbread Man?" the big, grizzly bear asked. The Gingerbread Man laughed as he raced past and said,

"I've outrun two road diggers, a man and his wife, and a little boy and I'll outrun you too-o-o!"

"Oh, you will, will you? We'll see about that!" growled the big, grizzly bear as he gave chase too.

But the Gingerbread Man only laughed louder, and ran faster, and soon he had outstripped them all again. He ran on until he met a wild wolf, sitting on a log deep in the wood. "Where are you going, Gingerbread Man?" the wolf asked.

The Gingerbread Man laughed as he raced past and said,

> "I've outrun a big, grizzly bear,
> two road diggers, a man and his wife,
> and a little boy and I'll outrun you
> too-o-o!"

"Oh, you will, will you? We'll see about that!" snarled the wild wolf as he gave chase too, but the Gingerbread Man only laughed louder, and ran faster and faster, and soon he had outstripped them all again.

The Gingerbread Man ran on until he met
a fox, who was lying basking in the sun.
"Where are you going, Gingerbread Man?"
the fox asked lazily without getting up.

The Gingerbread Man
laughed and said,

"I've outrun a wild wolf, a big grizzly bear,
two road diggers, a man and his wife, and a
little boy and I'll outrun you too-o-o!"

And the fox replied, "Sorry, Gingerbread Man, I can't quite hear
you. Won't you come a little closer?"
The Gingerbread Man paused briefly for the first time, and went
a bit closer to the fox and said proudly in a very loud voice,

"I've outrun a wild wolf, a big grizzly bear, two road diggers, a man and his wife, and a little boy and I'll outrun you too-o-o!"

"Sorry, I still can't quite hear you. Won't you come a little closer?" asked the fox in a feeble voice. The Gingerbread Man went right up to the fox, and leaning towards him yelled,

"I've outrun a wild wolf, a big grizzly bear, two road diggers, a man and his wife, and a little boy and I'll outrun you too-o-o!"

"Oh you will, will you? We'll see about that!" replied the fox, and –

SNAP!

– he snapped up the Gingerbread Man in his sharp teeth and gobbled him down just like that. And that was the end of the boastful Gingerbread Man, who could outrun the wild wolf, the big grizzly bear, the two road diggers, the man and his wife, and their little boy, but who couldn't outwit the wily fox.

CRY BABY BUNTING

Cry Baby Bunting,
Daddy's gone a hunting,
Gone to fetch a rabbit skin,
To wrap the Baby Bunting in.
Cry Baby Bunting.

DOCTOR FOSTER

Doctor Foster went to Gloucester,
In a shower of rain.

He stepped in a puddle,
Right up to his middle,
And never went there again.

WISE
OLD OWL

A wise old owl
lived in an oak.

The more he saw,
the less he spoke.
The less he spoke,
the more he heard.
Why can't we all be like that wise old bird?

MARY HAD
A LITTLE LAMB

Mary had a little lamb,
its fleece was white as snow,
And everywhere that Mary went,
the lamb was sure to go.

It followed her to school one day,
which was against the rule.
It made the children laugh and play,
to see a lamb at school.

And so the teacher turned it out,
but still it lingered near,
And waited patiently about
'til Mary did appear.

"Why does the lamb love Mary so?"
the eager children cry.
"Why Mary loves the lamb, you know,"
the teacher did reply.

LITTLE
MISS MUFFET

Little Miss Muffet sat on a tuffet,
Eating her curds and whey.

Along came a spider,
who sat down beside her,
And frightened Miss Muffet away.

LITTLE TOMMY TUCKER

Little Tommy Tucker, sings for his supper.
What shall we give him? Brown bread and butter.
How shall he cut it, without a knife?
How shall he marry, without a wife?

THREE
LITTLE PIGS

ONCE upon a time three little pigs set out to seek their fortune.

The first little pig met a man carrying a bundle of straw, and said to him, "Please will you let me have that bundle of straw to build a house?"

The day was hot and the man was tired with carrying the bundle of straw, so he was happy to hand it over. The little pig was delighted and set about building a house.

He had just finished, when a wolf came along, knocked at the door, and said, "Little pig, little pig, let me come in."

To which the little pig replied, "No, not by the hair on my chinny chin chin!"

"Then I'll huff, and I'll puff, and I'll blow your house in!" cried the angry wolf. So the wolf huffed, and he puffed, and he blew the house in, and he ate up the little pig.

The second little pig met a man with a bundle of sticks and said to him, "Please will you let me have that bundle of sticks to build a house?"

The man was in a hurry to get home for his dinner, so he happily handed over the bundle of sticks. The second little pig had only just moved into his house, when along came the wolf who said, "Little pig, little pig, let me come in."

To which the second little pig replied, "No, not by the hair on my chinny chin chin!"

"Then I'll huff, and I'll puff, and I'll blow your house in!" cried the angry wolf.

So he huffed, and he puffed, and he puffed, and he huffed, and at last he blew the house in, and he ate up the little pig.

The third little pig met a man with a load of bricks, and said to him, "Please will you let me have those bricks to build a house?" The bricks were very heavy, and the man's back ached, so he readily handed them over. The third little pig had just put the finishing touches to her house, when along came the wolf who said, "Little pig, little pig, let me come in."
To which the third little pig replied, "No, not by the hair on my chinny chin chin!"
"Then I'll huff, and I'll puff, and I'll blow your house in!" cried the wolf. So the wolf huffed, and he puffed, and he huffed and he puffed, and he puffed and huffed, but he could not blow the brick house in because it was too well built.

When he realized this, the wolf became very angry indeed, and declared he would climb down the chimney instead and eat up the little pig. But the clever third little pig was ready for him. She had made up a blazing fire and had put on a pot full of water to boil. When she heard the wolf scrabbling down the chimney, she took off the lid of the pot, and –

PLOP!

– in fell the wolf.

And before anyone could say, "Chinny chin chin!", the little pig had put the lid back on again. She boiled up the wolf and ate him for supper, and lived happily ever afterwards.

RIDE A COCK-HORSE

Ride a cock-horse to Banbury cross,
To see a fine lady upon a white horse.
With rings on her fingers and bells on her toes,
She shall have music wherever she goes.

INCY
WINCY
SPIDER

Incy Wincy Spider,
Climbing up the spout.
Down came the rain,
And washed the spider out.

Out came the sun,
And dried up all the rain.
Now Incy Wincy Spider,
Went up the spout again.

SIMPLE SIMON

Simple Simon met a pieman
going to the fair.
Said Simple Simon to the pieman,
"Let me taste your ware."

Said the pieman to Simple Simon,
"Show me first your penny."
Said Simple Simon to the pieman,
"Sir, I have not any!"

Simple Simon went a fishing
for to catch a whale;
All the water he had got
was in his mother's pail.

Simple Simon went to look
if plums grew on a thistle;
He pricked his fingers very much,
Which made poor Simon whistle.

He went for water in a sieve
but soon it all fell through;
And now poor Simple Simon
bids you all adieu.

JACK AND JILL

Jack and Jill went up the hill,
To fetch a pail of water.

Jack fell down and broke his crown,
And Jill came tumbling after.
Up Jack got, and home did trot,
As fast as he could caper.
He went to bed to mend his head,
With vinegar and brown paper.

GEORGIE
PORGIE

Georgie Porgie, pudding and pie,
Kissed the girls and made them cry.
When the boys came out to play,
Georgie Porgie ran away.

HUMPTY DUMPTY

Humpty Dumpty sat on a wall,
Humpty Dumpty had a great fall.
All the King's horses and all the King's men
Couldn't put Humpty together again.

LITTLE RED RIDING-HOOD

THERE was once a kind little girl, who was loved by everyone. Her grandmother made her a beautiful red riding-coat with a hood. The girl was so pleased with the coat that she wore it nearly all the time, and soon everyone called her Little Red Riding-Hood.

One day Little Red Riding-Hood's mother said, "Little Red
Riding-Hood, your grandma has been ill. Take her these cakes to
cheer her up. Go quickly and don't talk to anyone on your way!"
Little Red Riding-Hood set off at once and as she was skipping
along, she met a wolf. The wolf was so hungry that he was
tempted to eat her up there and then, but he dared not because
he could hear woodcutters nearby, so instead he stopped her
to ask her where she was going.

Forgetting what her mother had told her, Little Red Riding-Hood
said, "I am taking these cakes to my grandma who's been ill."
"Oh, dear. Does she live near here?" asked the wolf, pretending
to be kind.
"Yes, in a pretty little house in the middle of the wood," answered
Little Red Riding-Hood. The wolf said goodbye to her, and as
soon as she was out of sight, he ran as fast as he could towards
Grandma's cottage.

When the wolf arrived at Grandma's house, he knocked at the door – TAP, TAP, TAP, TAP.

"Who is there?" called Grandma.
"It's me, Little Red Riding-Hood," answered the wolf, disguising his voice. "I've brought you some cakes from Mama."
"Come in, Little Red Riding-Hood," called Grandma from her bed. "I have left the door on the latch."

The greedy wolf went in and –

GULP!

– gobbled down Grandma in one big mouthful, without even once chewing her.

He then quickly put on her spare bonnet, jumped into the bed and pulled the bedclothes up to his chin. He had scarcely settled himself, when there was another knock on the door – TAP, TAP, TAP, TAP.

"Who's there?" he called out.

Little Red Riding-Hood thought that her grandmother sounded a bit odd, but she decided her voice must be hoarse because she had been ill, so she answered, "It's me, Little Red Riding-Hood. I've brought you some cakes from Mama."

Softening his voice as much as he could, the wolf called out, "Come in, Little Red Riding-Hood. I have left the door on the latch."

Little Red Riding-Hood went in, but seeing how strange her grandmother looked, she said, "Grandma, what huge ears you have!"

"All the better to hear you with, my dear."

"Grandma, what big eyes you have!"

"All the better to see you with, my dear."

"Grandma, what sharp teeth you have!"

"All the better to EAT you with, my dear."

And with these words, the wicked wolf fell upon poor Little Red Riding-Hood, and ate her up in one big

GULP!

Having satisfied his hunger, the wolf fell asleep, and was soon snoring loudly –
zzzzzzzz! ZZZZZZZ! ZZZZZZZZ!

In fact he snored so loudly that a hunter passing the house decided to go in to see if something was wrong. When he saw the sleeping wolf, the hunter cried, "Aha! I have been looking for you for a long time, you rascal!"

He quickly chopped off the wolf's head and out jumped Little Red Riding-Hood, followed by her grandmother. So all ended well. The hunter had his wolf, Grandma ate the cakes and felt a lot better, and Little Red Riding-Hood said she would never, ever stop and talk to a strange wolf ever again.

AS I WAS GOING TO ST.IVES

As I was going to St.Ives,
I met a man with seven wives.
Each wife had seven sacks,
And in each sack were seven cats.
Each cat had seven kits.
Kits, cats, sacks, wives,
How many were going to St.Ives?

DING DONG BELL

Ding dong bell,
Pussy's in the well.
Who put her in?
Little Johnny Flynn.

Who pulled her out?
Little Tommy Stout.
What a naughty boy was that,
Try to drown poor pussy cat,
Who never did him any harm,
But killed all the mice in the Farmer's barn!

RAIN, RAIN, GO AWAY

Rain, rain, go away,
Come again another day.
Little Johnny wants to play.
Rain, rain, go to Spain,
never show your face again.

FOR THE
WANT OF A NAIL

For want of a nail
The shoe was lost,
For want of a shoe
The horse was lost,
For want of a horse
The rider was lost,

For want of a rider
The battle was lost,
For want of a battle
The kingdom was lost,
And all for the want of a nail.

GOOSEY GOOSEY GANDER

Goosey Goosey Gander,
Where shall I wander?

Upstairs, downstairs,
In my lady's chamber.
There I met an old man,
Who wouldn't say his prayers.
I took him by the left leg,
And threw him down the stairs.

BAA BAA BLACK SHEEP

Baa baa black sheep, have you any wool?
Yes sir, yes sir, three bags full.
One for the master, one for the dame,
And one for the little boy who lives down the lane.

GOLDILOCKS AND THE THREE BEARS

ONCE upon a time there was a little girl who had such pretty, blonde hair that everyone called her Goldilocks. One day she was walking in the woods when she came across a little house. She knocked on the door, and when no one answered, she went inside.

Now, the house belonged to a family of bears. There was a great big bear, a middle-sized bear and a little baby bear. The great big bear had made them some porridge and poured it into three bowls: a great big one, a middle-sized one and a tiny one for baby bear. The porridge had been too hot to eat, so the bears had decided to go out for a walk while it cooled down.

133

When Goldilocks saw the three steaming bowls of delicious-looking porridge on the table, her tummy began to rumble.

"I'll just have a little taste," she thought. "There is no one about, and I am sure that they wouldn't mind."

So first she took a spoonful from the great big bowl. "Much too salty!" she cried in disgust.

Then she tried a spoonful from the middle-sized bowl. "Much too sweet!" she decided.

Finally she tried the tiny bowl. "Just right!" she said happily, and she ate it all up.

By now Goldilocks was feeling a bit tired. Near the table there were three chairs: a great big one, a middle-sized one and a tiny one. She sat down on the great big one.

"Much too high!" she declared, jumping up quickly.

Next she tried the middle-sized one. "Much too low!" she said.

Finally she tried the tiny one. "Just right!" she said happily, and she sat down on it. But really she was far too big for little baby bear's chair. The leg broke, and with a terrible –

CRASH!

– Goldilocks tumbled to the floor.

"Bother!" she said, and she stomped up the stairs. In the bedroom she found three beds: a great big one, a middle-sized one and a tiny one. First she tried the great big one. "Much too hard!" she decided. Next she tried the middle-sized one. "Too soft!" she declared. Finally she tried the tiny one. "Just right!" she said happily, and she climbed in, pulled up the covers and was soon fast asleep.

Meanwhile the three bears had returned from their walk, and they were ready for their porridge. First the great big one looked at his bowl and said in his great big cross voice,

"Someone has been eating my porridge!"

Then the middle-sized one looked at her bowl and said in her middle-sized voice,

"Someone has been eating my porridge!"

Finally little baby bear looked at his bowl and said in his little baby voice,

"Someone has been eating my porridge, and what's more, they have eaten it all up!"

Then the great big bear looked at his chair and said in his great big voice,

"Someone has been sitting in my chair!"

So the middle-sized bear went and looked at her chair and said in her middle-sized voice,

"Someone has been sitting in my chair too!"

So little baby bear looked at his chair and said
in his little baby voice,

"Someone has been sitting in my chair, and what's more, they have broken it all to bits!"

Then the three bears went upstairs. The great big bear looked at his rumpled bed and cried out in his great big voice,

"Someone has been lying in my bed!"

So the middle-sized bear looked at her bed and said in her middle-sized voice,

"Someone has been lying in my bed!"

The little baby bear looked at his bed.

"Someone has been lying in my bed!" he cried. "And what's more . . .

. . . they are still there!"

With that, Goldilocks woke up. When she saw the three cross bears looking at her, she was very frightened indeed.

She raced down the stairs and out of the house, and didn't stop running until she reached home, and that was the very last time that she ever ate someone's porridge without asking them first!

THE MAN IN THE
WILDERNESS

The man in the wilderness asked me,
"How many strawberries grow in the sea?"
I answered him as I thought good,
"As many as herrings grow in the wood."

PAT-A-CAKE, PAT-A-CAKE

Pat-a-cake, Pat-a-cake, baker's man,

Bake me a cake as fast as you can.

Pat it and prick it, and mark it with a 'B',

And put it in the oven for baby and me.

ONE, TWO, BUCKLE MY SHOE

1, 2,
buckle my shoe,

3, 4,
shut the door,

5, 6,
pick up sticks,

7, 8,
lay them straight,

9, 10,
a good fat hen.

LITTLE BOY BLUE

Little Boy Blue
come blow your horn,
The sheep's in the meadow,
the cow's in the corn.

But where is the boy
who looks after the sheep?
He's under a haystack fast asleep.
Will you wake him?
No, not I,
For if I do, he's sure to cry.

ROCK-A-BYE
BABY

Rock-a-bye baby on the tree top,
When the wind blows, the cradle will rock.
When the bough breaks, the cradle will fall,
And down will come baby, cradle and all.

TOM, THE PIPER'S SON

Tom he was a piper's son,
He learned to play when he was young.
But all the tunes that he could play
Was "Over the hills and far away."

JACK AND THE BEANSTALK

ONCE upon a time a poor widow lived with her son, Jack. The only thing of any value that they owned was a cow, but the cow was growing old, and eventually it had no milk to give. "There's nothing for it, Jack," said the widow sadly. "You'll have to sell the cow."

So Jack set off to market. He hadn't gone far when he met
a strange old man, who said to him, "Good morning, Jack.
Where are you off to?"
"I'm going to the market to sell our cow," Jack replied.
"I'll tell you what, I'll give you this magic bean in exchange for
her and save you the bother," said the old man. "Plant it tonight
and by morning it will have grown right up to the sky!"
So Jack gave him the cow, took the bean and set off home.

When Jack's poor mother discovered that he had been such a fool,
she was very angry. She threw the bean out of the window and
sent him to bed without any supper.

The next morning when Jack woke up, his room was so dark that at first he thought that it must still be night-time. But when he looked out, he realized that the bean his mother had thrown into the garden had sprung up into a HUGE beanstalk, which went

up ...and up ...and up

until it reached the sky!

Jack jumped onto the beanstalk and

climbed...

and **climbed**...

and climbed

...and climbed

... until at last he reached the top.

When he got there, he walked along a road until he came to an enormous house, outside of which sat an enormous woman.

"Good morning! Would you be so kind as to give me some breakfast?" Jack asked her politely.

"Be off with you!" replied the enormous woman. "Or it's breakfast you yourself will be!

My husband is an ogre, and there's nothing he likes better than baked boys on toast for his breakfast!"

"Oh, please, give me something to eat! I've had nothing since yesterday morning," pleaded Jack, "so I may as well be baked on toast as die of hunger!"

The ogre's wife took Jack into the kitchen, and gave him a hunk of stale bread. Jack had just opened his mouth to take a bite, when –

THUMP! THUMP! THUMP! – the whole house began to tremble.

"Goodness, it's my husband!" said the ogre's wife. "Quick, jump in here!" And she bundled Jack into a cupboard, just as an enormous ogre waddled into the room. He looked around suspiciously and bellowed,

"Fee-fi-fo-fum, I smell the blood of an Englishman!"

"Nonsense, dear," said his wife. "You're dreaming. Come and have your breakfast."

When the ogre had finished his breakfast – and a noisy business that was too – he took a large bag of gold out of a chest and began to count it. But soon his head started to nod and he began to snore until the whole house shook.

Then Jack nervously crept out of the cupboard, took the bag of gold and ran as fast as he could until he came to the beanstalk. He threw the bag of gold down into his mother's garden below, and then he climbed down and down the beanstalk until at last he was safely back home.

Jack and his mother spent the gold wisely, but eventually it ran out, and there was no food left. Rather than see his mother starve, Jack bravely decided to climb the beanstalk one more time, so up and up he climbed and at last he reached the top. He walked along the road until he came to the great big house, and there standing outside it as before was the ogre's wife.

"Good morning!" said Jack. "Would you be so kind as to give me some breakfast?"

The ogre's wife didn't recognize Jack, so she took him in and gave him a crust of bread. But scarcely had he taken a bite when –

THUMP!
   THUMP!
      THUMP!

– they heard the ogre's footsteps approaching.

His wife bundled Jack into the cupboard just as the enormous ogre strode into the room, bellowing,

"Fee-fi-fo-fum, I smell the blood of an Englishman!"

Then, just as before, his wife distracted the ogre by giving him his breakfast. When he had finished, he said, "Wife, bring me the hen that lays the golden eggs." So she brought it, and the ogre said, "Lay," and the hen laid an egg of solid gold. Soon the ogre's head started to nod and he began to snore until the whole house shook again.

Then Jack crept out of the cupboard and picked up the golden hen. He was just racing out of the door with it, when the hen went – CLUCK! CLUCK! – and woke the ogre, who gave chase. But Jack was too fast for him. He ran as fast as he could until he came to the beanstalk. He climbed down and down the beanstalk, until at last he was safely back home.

Jack and his mother were very pleased with the hen, but eventually it stopped laying eggs. Jack was terrified of taking on the ogre again, but he hated seeing his mother so hungry, so there was nothing else for it. Once more he jumped onto the beanstalk, and climbed and climbed until he reached the top.

When he got near to the ogre's house, Jack waited until he saw the ogre's wife come out.

Then he crept into the house and hid in a basket of washing. He had just covered himself up, when he heard –

THUMP! THUMP! THUMP!

– and in came the ogre and his wife.

"Fee-fi-fo-fum, I smell the blood of an Englishman!"

the ogre bellowed in rage.

"Well," said the ogre's wife, "if it's that little rogue who was here before, then he'll be in the cupboard."

They both rushed to the cupboard, but, of course, luckily Jack wasn't there this time. So the ogre sat down to breakfast. When he had finished, he called out, "Wife, bring me my golden harp." Then he said: "Sing!" and the golden harp sang and it went on singing until the ogre fell asleep, and began to snore, and the whole house shook again.

Then Jack bravely crept out from under the washing, grabbed the harp and dashed out of the door. The ogre woke up and lumbered after him, bellowing with rage.

When he got to the beanstalk, Jack climbed down and down just as fast as he could. The ogre swung himself on to the beanstalk, and began climbing down after him.

As he neared the bottom, Jack called out, "Mother! Mother! Bring me an axe!" His mother came rushing out with the axe, but froze with fright when she saw the ogre. Jack jumped down, took hold of the axe and gave the beanstalk a mighty – CHOP! – which cut it in two. The ogre tumbled down – so that was the end of him – and the beanstalk came toppling after.

So Jack's bravery was rewarded. He travelled round the country
with his magic harp and soon became famous. He and his mother
managed to buy their cow back from the strange old man,
and the three of them lived happily ever after
and never wanted for another thing.

LITTLE ROBIN REDBREAST

Little Robin Redbreast sat upon a tree,
Up went Pussy, and down went he:
Down came Pussy, and away Robin ran:
Says Little Robin Redbreast, "Catch me if you can."
Little Robin Redbreast jumped upon a wall,
Pussy jumped after him and almost got a fall;
Little Robin chirped and sang, and what did Pussy say?
Pussy said "Miaow!" and Robin jumped away.

PETER PIPER

Peter Piper picked a peck of pickled pepper.
A peck of pickled pepper Peter Piper picked.
If Peter Piper picked a peck of pickled pepper,
Where's the peck of pickled pepper
Peter Piper picked?

THERE WAS AN OLD WOMAN WHO LIVED IN A SHOE

There was an old woman who lived in a shoe,
She had so many children she didn't know what to do.
She gave them some broth, without any bread,
And she whipped them all soundly and sent them to bed!

HEY DIDDLE DIDDLE

Hey diddle diddle,
the cat and the fiddle,
The cow jumped
over the moon.
The little dog laughed
to see such fun,
And the dish ran away
with the spoon.

INDEX OF FIRST LINES